W9-AYK-549

Coco
the carrot

written and illustrated by
Steven Salerno

MARSHALL CAVENDISH
NEW YORK ✿ LONDON ✿ SINGAPORE

Marshall Cavendish, 99 White Plains Road, Tarrytown, NY 10591
www.marshallcavendish.us
Library of Congress Cataloging-in-Publication Data
Salerno, Steven.
Coco the Carrot / written and illustrated by Steven Salerno.— 1st ed.
p. cm.
Summary: Tired of life in the refrigerator, Coco the Carrot sets off for Paris
to become a famous hat designer.
ISBN 0-7614-5191-9
[1. Carrots—Fiction. 2. Hats—Fiction.] I. Title.
PZ7.S15212Co 2002
[E]—dc21
2001022035
The text of this book is set in Bernhard Modern.
The illustrations are rendered in watercolor and gouache.
Printed in China
First edition
1 2 4 6 5 3

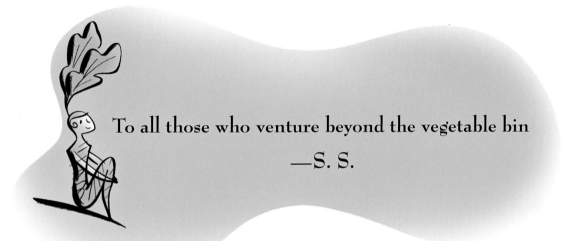

To all those who venture beyond the vegetable bin

—S. S.

Coco the Carrot lived in a cold, cramped vegetable bin.
She didn't like it one bit.

None of the other vegetables liked it either, but they were too afraid to leave.

Coco was different.

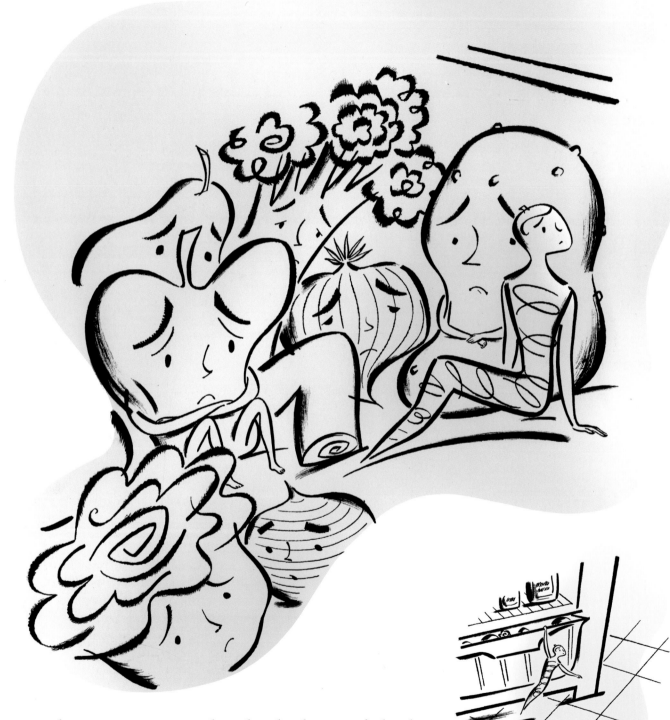

Early one morning she climbed out of the bin. "Good-bye," Coco whispered.

In the next room she found a sewing basket
and made herself a beautiful green hat.

"Splendid! *Now* I am ready to see the world," said Coco,
admiring herself in the mirror.

She rode the elevator down to the lobby. The doorman hailed a taxi, and Coco hopped into the backseat.

"Where to?" asked the driver.

"Paris!" shouted Coco.

"I can't take you there myself, but I can take you to a ship that leaves for Paris today, OK?"

"Perfect!" said Coco.

So off they drove to the pier. The taxi screeched to a stop.

The ship's whistle blew loudly. whhhooooooooooogg!

"All aboard for Paris!" called the captain.
Coco scurried up the gangway, the last one to board.
The great ship sailed out of the harbor.

Coco was shown to a cabin with a little round window overlooking the ocean.

"This will do nicely," she said.

That evening at dinner, Coco was invited to sit with the captain and his other guests. Although none of them had ever met a carrot before, they found Coco to be charming and witty.

"Tell me, Coco, my dear, what is it that you do?"
asked an elegant woman.

"Well, I . . . I . . . made this hat," answered Coco politely.

"Ahhh, so you are a hat designer," exclaimed the captain.

"Yes! I guess I am," said Coco.

"It is a FABULOUS hat! Could you make one for me?"
asked the elegant woman.

"Yes, of course," replied Coco. "I'll make new hats for all of you!"

Coco wrote down their names and addresses on a slip of paper,
put it in her pocket, and promised to make their hats as soon as she
arrived in Paris.

One afternoon Coco sat in a deck chair reading a book.
Suddenly a cook stepped onto the deck.
He glared at Coco. It made her nervous!

"I know what you are," snapped the cook. "You're just a carrot that belongs in my soup!"

"I'm going to *Paris*," Coco said.

"No, you're not!" yelled the cook and chased poor Coco all around the ship's deck.

Coco hid behind one of the lifeboats,
her heart thumping.
   "Where are you, my tasty little carrot?"
sneered the cook. He spotted Coco's green
hat and made a grab for her.
   Coco leaped aside . . .
   and fell through the ship's railing.
   She splashed into the ocean far below!

   "Help me! Help me!" she cried, but no one could hear
her tiny voice.
   Coco clung to a piece of driftwood as the huge ship
moved slowly away.

Coco's teeth chattered, and the icy waves
tossed her all about.

It was a long, lonely night. Coco wished she had never
left her vegetable bin!

The following morning the waves were calm,
and the ocean sparkled in the sun.

Coco washed ashore on a beautiful tropical island.
"It's so exotic!" she exclaimed.

Coco explored and met a friendly monkey.

The monkey's name was Anton.
He showed Coco how to climb a coconut tree,
and Coco showed Anton how to play shuffleboard.
Together they made a home out of sticks
with a roof of palm leaves to keep
them dry when it rained.
    They became the best of friends.

During the day they swam in the
ocean and played on the beach.
    At night Coco sang, and Anton
danced around the fire.

Although Coco had not made it to Paris,
she wanted to keep her promise to make
hats for all the friends she had met on the ship.

Coco began to make a different style hat for each name
on her list.
She used leaves, grass, vines, bark, flowers, shells,
and pieces of sailcloth Anton had found washed up on the beach.

Each hat Coco created was more beautiful than the last.

Anton made hatboxes out of bamboo.
He placed a hat inside each box and tied down
the lid with a vine. On the outside of the lid Coco wrote a name
and address from her list, and on the bottom she wrote:
HATS BY COCO—TROPICAL ISLE.

Together, Coco and Anton placed all of the hatboxes
in the ocean. They watched the tide carry them away.
"Thank you, Anton, for all your help," said Coco.
She gave him a handsome blue hat as a gift.

The bamboo hatboxes floated to cities all around the world.
Everyone on the list received a hat from Coco.
When the captain received his hat he said, "Aye, aye!"
Soon, many other people saw these hats and wanted one, too.
"We want hats made by Coco!" they all cried.

They sent letters and e-mail to the largest hat factory in the world,
located in Paris, and demanded hats made by "Coco."

"Who is this Coco?" asked Mademoiselle Chapeau,
the owner of the hat factory.
"I must find her! She *must* come to Paris and create hats for me.
I will make her *famous*!"

Mademoiselle Chapeau had one of the bamboo hatboxes delivered to her office. She put on her glasses and examined the box carefully.

"Ahhh-Haaa!" she cried.

On the bottom of the box, in tiny letters, was written: HATS BY COCO—TROPICAL ISLE.

Mademoiselle Chapeau immediately hired an airplane and set off to find the mysterious and talented Coco.

She searched every tropical island in the world, but Coco was nowhere to be found. Just as Mademoiselle Chapeau was about to give up, the pilot said he knew of a small tropical island that wasn't on any map.

"Take me there, NOW!" ordered Mademoiselle Chapeau.

Coco and Anton were gathering coconuts when they spotted the airplane circling over their island.

The pilot landed the plane on the beach.

"Are *you* Coco, the hat designer?" asked Mademoiselle Chapeau, a bit surprised to see a carrot.

"Yes," said Coco, "I am."

"I'm here to take you to Paris. Design hats for me, and I will make you famous!" exclaimed Mademoiselle Chapeau.

"Paris?" asked Coco. "Anton, we are going to *Paris*!"

So off they flew, through the night, all the way to Paris.

Mademoiselle Chapeau found an apartment for Coco and Anton in a wonderful old building. Coco painted a picture of a palm tree on the wall. Anton felt right at home swinging from the chandelier.

The very next day Mademoiselle Chapeau brought Coco and Anton to the hat factory. She introduced them to all the helpers.

Coco started work immediately on sketches for new hats.
Mademoiselle Chapeau placed Anton in charge of all the machines.

Giant rolls of fabric arrived in trucks. A hundred helpers
cut and sewed the fabric, adding bows, bangles, buttons, beads,
ribbons, feathers, and lace. So many sewing machines were all
working at once that the factory sounded like a giant bumblebee.

At the far end of the factory, each hat was placed into a hatbox.
Then the boxes were loaded onto trucks, delivered to the airport,
and flown to hat shops around the world.

All the hat shop owners placed large
signs in their front windows. They read:
HATS BY COCO!
The hat shops quickly filled with
new customers.

Soon it seemed everyone was wearing one of Coco's fabulous new hats.

After work each day, Coco and Anton walked
through the streets of Paris, taking in all the sights.

Day after day, hundreds of
hats were made at the factory.
Coco was busy drawing new hat
designs, while Mademoiselle Chapeau
paced back and forth on the factory floor.

Reporters from magazines, newspapers, and
television visited the factory to interview the talented
Coco the Carrot.

One evening the Hat Society of Paris held a spectacular Gala Ball in honor of Coco. Hat shop owners from all over the world flew to Paris to attend.

Anton received the Silver Medallion for his special skills. Coco was presented with the Golden Hat Award for her many beautiful hat designs. The mayor of Paris kissed Coco on both cheeks. The people attending the Gala Ball cheered, whistled, and clapped. Mademoiselle Chapeau was so proud!

Everyone danced late into the night.

After the ball, Coco and Anton walked home together. Coco noticed that Anton looked sad.

When they returned to their apartment, Anton sat up in the chandelier, his tail drooping.

"Do you miss our tropical island?" Coco asked her friend.

Anton nodded tearfully.

"I do, too," said Coco.

The very next morning Coco said good-bye
to Mademoiselle Chapeau.
"We're homesick for our tropical island," she explained.
Mademoiselle Chapeau was very sad to see Coco and Anton leave.
Coco promised to visit her once a year and bring new hat designs.

At the airport hundreds of people had gathered to say good-bye.
Mademoiselle Chapeau kissed Coco and Anton on both cheeks
and presented them with their very own airplane.
"Au revoir, Paris! Merci beaucoup!" Coco shouted to the crowd.
Anton started the engine. The propeller whirred.
He guided the plane down the runway and up into the sky.

Anton looped their new plane twice
around the Eiffel Tower and headed home.

The next morning they arrived back at their tropical island, safe and sound.

During the day they swam in the ocean and played on the beach. At night Coco sang, and Anton danced around the fire, just as before.

Coco and Anton are still there today.
Sometimes Coco makes a new hat just for the fun of it.
Anton places it in a bamboo hatbox and ties down the lid with a vine.

Together they place the hatbox in the ocean
and watch the tide carry it away.

So don't be surprised if one day you find a bamboo
hatbox on your doorstep. Inside will be a beautiful hat
made by Coco the Carrot.